Stories of Ponies

Rosie Dickins

Illustrated by
Peter Kavanagh

Reading consultant: Alison Kelly
Roehampton University
Horse and pony consultant: Juliet Penwarden, BHSII

Contents

Chapter 1

Pony magic

Magic put her head over the stall door and whinnied.

Molly smiled. "It's the show today," she said. "Let's see if we can win something this time!"

"Still daydreaming about ribbons and rosettes?" laughed Dad. He was helping Molly get ready. "You'll need a touch of magic for that!" And he laughed so much, he tripped over a box of brushes.

CRASH!

Magic trembled all over. She didn't like sudden noises. It was hard to see how she would win anything at a noisy show. But Molly was determined to try.

Molly brushed Magic's coat until it shone. Then she combed the pony's tail and oiled her hooves.

The showground was
crowded with eager riders and
excited ponies. Molly did her
best to keep Magic calm.

Their first competition was the dressing-up race. Heaps of clothes waited at the start. You raced to the clothes, put them on and led your pony back to the finish.

But Molly's race didn't go
according to plan...

Next came the box race. For this, riders raced to collect boxes and stack them up together.

Molly and Magic got off to a good start. But then...

"Never mind," Molly said,
trying not to sound too
disappointed. "There's still
the flag race."

Molly and Magic were
waiting to start the flag race
when, suddenly, there was a
loud noise.

It was only a burst balloon –
but it was too much for
Magic. She cleared the fence
around the ring in one bound.

12

Dad was watching in the crowd. "That was a beautiful jump," he told Molly. "Maybe you should try a different competition."

Dad led Molly and Magic to another ring. "A late entry," he told the surprised steward.

"What do I do?" whispered Molly nervously.

"Just keep calm and steer Magic around the jumps," Dad replied. "She knows how to do the rest."

Molly looked at the jumps. Each one had a number showing which order to jump them in. "Ready, Magic?" she whispered, touching her heels to the pony's sides. Magic set off eagerly.

They soared over
the first jump...

and the
second...

and the
third.

There were seven jumps in all.
Magic cleared every single one
without a fault.

There was a burst of applause.
Dad was clapping loudest of all.
"You've won!" he cried.

Well done!

Molly leaned down and
patted Magic. "Now that was
real magic," she said proudly.

Chapter 2

The naughtiest pony

"No, Rascal!" shouted Becky. "Don't eat the flowers." She tied him up, away from the flower pots, and went to get a brush.

Becky got back just in time
to see Rascal pulling the
knot undone.

Bad Rascal!

Rascal was the naughtiest
pony she had ever met. But he
was so much fun, she could never
stay cross with him for long.

Just then, Aunt Elspeth
appeared. "Thanks for taking
care of that pony," she called.
"He's such a
handful!"

"Once you've finished, how
about coming for a ride with
me?" she added.

"Yes please!" said Becky. She
loved riding Rascal – and her
aunt knew all the best paths
and bridleways.

Soon, she and Rascal were clattering out of the yard behind Elspeth and her big red mare, Rocket. They rode slowly along quiet lanes until they came to a grassy field.

"Let's try a canter," said Aunt Elspeth, letting Becky go ahead. Becky sat deep in the saddle and touched her legs to Rascal's sides. He raced off, his hooves thudding on the grass.

When they got back,
Becky let Rascal into the
field. He trotted over to a big
patch of mud and had a
good roll, his hooves waving
happily in the air.

23

Back in the tack room, Becky began polishing Rascal's saddle. Outside, Aunt Elspeth started the car. "I'm going to get more hay," she called.

Suddenly, there was a squeal of brakes and a frightened whinny. Rascal! Becky ran out.

There on the corner was her aunt's car – with Rascal standing just in front of it.

"What's this pony doing on the road?" shouted Aunt Elspeth. "He could have been hurt!" She turned to Becky. "You didn't shut the gate to the field!"

Aunt Elspeth led Rascal back to the stable yard and tied him up by the tack room. Then she turned to Becky. "You'd better leave," she said sharply. "And don't come back until you learn to shut gates!"

Becky flushed. "I did shut the gate," she said.

"Then how did Rascal get out?" her aunt snapped. Becky had no answer.

Becky set off home, trying not to cry. She felt awful when she thought about Rascal's narrow escape. And she felt even worse about not riding him any more.

"I might as well throw away my riding hat," she sniffed. "Oh no – my hat!" It was still in the tack room. She would have to go back and get it.

Rascal was still standing by the tack room, looking rather pleased with himself. And a banging noise was coming from inside. Puzzled, Becky unlocked the door...

...and Aunt Elspeth burst out. "Thank goodness," she sighed.

"Wh-what happened?" Becky stammered.

"Rascal locked me in!" her
aunt explained. "He can move
bolts with his teeth. He must
have let himself out of the
field, too."

Becky felt a wave of relief.

"I'm sorry I blamed you," her aunt added. "I've never known such a rascally pony!"

Becky smiled. "But he got *me* out of trouble," she thought to herself. "Maybe he's not such a rascal after all."

Chapter 3

The littlest pony

"Hey shrimp," shouted Marco, "pass me my hat."

"Don't call me that," snapped Sally, throwing it over.

Sally hated the nickname – just as she hated being the smallest rider at the riding school. Marco, her brother, was always teasing her about her size.

"It's all right for him," she muttered to Sugar, the Shetland pony she was leading out to the field. "He can ride all the big ponies."

"I've only got you... and now no one can ride you because you're having a baby."

The little Shetland snuffled gently in reply. Her sides were big and round. The foal was due any day.

Sally left Sugar grazing happily and walked back.

Kate, who ran the school, was standing in the stable yard. "Can you give me a hand mucking out?" she asked.

Sally sighed. "Of course," she replied.

Mucking out took ages...

and then they had to refill the water buckets...

and sweep the stable yard.

By lunchtime, Sally was exhausted, but the stable yard was spotless.

Where's Marco?

The morning ride arrived back in a clatter of hooves. "Having a nice day, Cinders?" yelled Marco, as he jumped down from his pony.

Sally flung her broom into
a corner. "We'll be late home
for lunch," she said crossly.

"No we won't — not if we
cut through the field," Marco
answered.

Halfway across the field, Sally stopped. "Where's Sugar?" she asked. "She's vanished!"

Then they heard a faint whinny. "Sugar!" cried Sally. "It came from those bushes," Marco said. "Let's go and look."

The bushes were very tangled. They could just see Sugar through a small gap. Her halter was caught on a branch.

"I bet she was looking for apples," said Marco.

"And now she's stuck," Sally cried. "We've got to help her!"

Marco tried to squeeze in after Sugar – but there wasn't enough room.

Then Sally tried. Ignoring the scratches, she pushed her way between the branches.

"Lucky you're so small," said Marco.

Sally unhooked the halter and coaxed Sugar out. Then she led the trembling pony back to the stable yard.

Marco told Kate what had happened, while Sally put Sugar back in her stall.

The next day, Sally and
Marco went to see how Sugar
was doing.

Kate was standing by
Sugar's stall with the vet.
"Oh no," cried Sally,
breaking into a run.

"It's ok," laughed Kate. "Look!"

There, lying in the straw beside her mother, was the smallest pony Sally had ever seen. She had big, dark eyes and a beautiful cinnamon-brown coat.

"We were wondering what to call her," Kate told Sally. "What do you think?"

"How about Spice?" Sally said, looking at the foal's coat.

"Good idea," agreed Kate.

Sugar and Spice, and all things nice!

Sugar stood up to say hello to
Sally. Spice struggled up too.
Her legs were very wobbly.

"She's lovely," said Marco,
looking over Sally's shoulder.
"Well, small is beautiful!"
Sally said happily.

Series Editor: Lesley Sims

Designed by Katarina Dragoslavić

Cover design by Russell Punter

This edition first published in 2007 by Usborne Publishing Ltd.,
Usborne House, 83-85 Saffron Hill, London EC1N 8RT, England.
www.usborne.com
Copyright © 2007, 2005 Usborne Publishing Ltd.

48